NURSERY & PLAYTIME Rhymes

Illustrated by Wendy Straw

Sandy Creek

Illustrations by Wendy Straw

Sandy Creek
122 Fifth Avenue
New York, NY 10011

ISBN: 978-1-4351-1813-3

Printed and bound in China

1 3 5 7 9 10 8 6 4 2

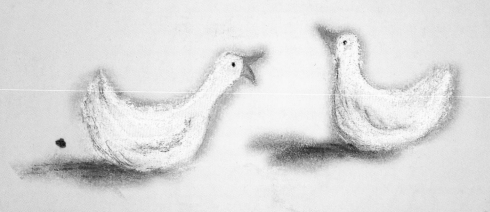

CONTENTS

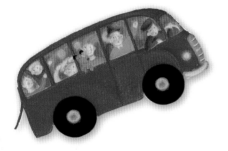

Peter Peter Pumpkin Eater

Peter, **Peter**, pumpkin eater,
Had a wife and couldn't keep her.
He put her in a **pumpkin** shell
And there he kept her very well.

The Wheels on the Bus

The wheels on the bus
Go round and round,
Round and round,
Round and round,

The wheels on the bus
Go round and round . . .

All day long . . .

The driver on the bus
Goes beep, beep, beep,
Beep, beep, beep,
Beep, beep, beep,

The driver on the bus
Goes beep, beep, beep . . .

All day long . . .

9

The people on the bus
go up and down,
Up and down,
Up and down,

10

The people on the bus
Go up and down . . .

All day long . . .

The wipers on the bus
Go swish, swish, swish,
Swish, swish, swish,
Swish, swish, swish,

The wipers on the bus
Go swish, swish, swish . . .

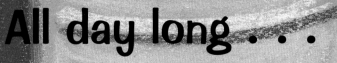

All day long . . . .

The wheels on the bus
Go round and round,
Round and round,
Round and round,

14

The wheels on the bus
Go round and round,

Bus Depot

Until the day is gone.

Humpty Dumpty

Humpty **Dumpty** sat on the wall.
Humpty **Dumpty** had
a great *fall* . . .

All the king's horses and all the king's men
Couldn't put **Humpty** together again!

17

Old MacDonald Had a Farm

Old MacDonald had a farm,
Ee-I Ee-I Oh,

And on that farm he had some ducks,
Ee-I Ee-I Oh,

With a Quack! Quack! here, and a Quack! Quack there,
Here a Quack! There a Quack! Everywhere a Quack! Quack!
Old MacDonald had a farm,
Ee-I Ee-I Oh!

Quack!

And on that farm he had some cows,
Ee-I Ee-I Oh,

With a **Moo! Moo!** here, and a **Moo! Moo!** there,
Here a **Moo!** There a **Moo!** Everywhere a **Moo! Moo!**
Old MacDonald had a farm,
Ee-I Ee-I Oh!

And on that farm he had some pigs,
Ee-I Ee-I Oh,

With an **Oink! Oink!** here, and an **Oink! Oink!** there,
Here an **Oink!** There an **Oink!** Everywhere an **Oink! Oink!**
Old MacDonald had a farm,
Ee-I Ee-I Oh!

Oink!

Oink!

Oink!

And on that farm he had some sheep,
Ee-I Ee-I Oh,

With a **Baa! Baa!** here, and a **Baa! Baa!** there,
Here a **Baa!** There a **Baa!** Everywhere a **Baa! Baa!**
Old MacDonald had a farm,
Ee-I Ee-I Oh!

Baa!

Baa!

Baa!

Baa!

With a **Quack! Quack!** here, and a **Moo! Moo!** there,

Moo!

Oink!

Oink!

Baa!

Baa!

26

Here an **Oink!** There an Oink! Everywhere a **Baa! Baa!**

Old MacDonald had a farm,

Ee-I Ee-I Oh!

Baa, Baa, Black Sheep

Baa Baa's Wool Shop

Baa, baa, black sheep,
Have you any wool?
Yes sir, yes sir,
Three bags full!

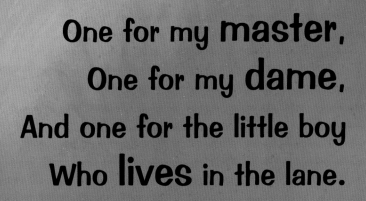

One for my **master**,
One for my **dame**,
And one for the little boy
Who **lives** in the lane.

Five Little Ducks

5 little ducks went out one day
over the hills and far away,

Mother duck called

Quack! **Quack!**

Quack! Quack!

But only four little ducks came back.

4 little ducks went out one day
over the hills and far away,

Mother duck called

Quack! **Quack!**

Quack! Quack!

But only three little ducks came back.

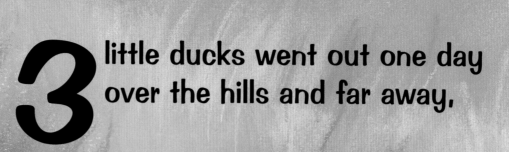

3 little ducks went out one day
over the hills and far away,

Mother duck called

Quack! **Quack!**

Quack! Quack!

But only two little ducks came back.

**2** little ducks went out one day
over the hills and far away,

Mother duck called

Quack! **Quack!**

Quack! Quack!

But only one little duck came back.

1 little duck went out one day
over the hills and far away,

Mother duck called

Quack! **Quack!**

Quack! Quack!

And all her five little ducks came back.

Here We Go Round the Mulberry Bush

Here we go round the mulberry bush,
The mulberry bush, the mulberry bush.
Here we go round the mulberry bush,
So early in the morning.

This is the way we wash our clothes,
Wash our clothes, wash our clothes.
This is the way we wash our clothes,
So early Monday morning.

This is the way we iron our clothes,
Iron our clothes,
    iron our clothes.
This is the way we
    iron our clothes,
So early Tuesday morning.

This is the way we mend our clothes
Mend our clothes, mend our clothes,
This is the way we mend our clothes
So early Wednesday morning.

This is the way we **sweep** the floor,
Sweep the floor, sweep the floor.
This is the way we sweep the floor,
So early Thursday morning.

This is the way we **scrub** the floor,
Scrub the floor, scrub the floor.
This is the way we scrub the floor,
So early Friday morning.

This is the way we **bake** our bread,
Bake our bread, bake our bread.
This is the way we bake our bread,
So early Saturday morning.

This is the way we **play** together,
Play together, play together.
This is the way we play together,
So early Sunday morning.

Itsy Bitsy Spider

Itsy Bitsy spider climbed up the water spout,
Down came the rain and washed the spider out.

Out came the sunshine and dried up all the rain,
so Itsy Bitsy spider climbed up the spout again.

Old King Cole

Old King Cole was a merry old soul,
And a merry old soul was he.
He called for his pipe and he called for his bowl,
And he called for his fiddlers three.

Every **fiddler** he had a fiddle,

And a very fine fiddle had he,

Oh there's none so **rare**, as can compare

With King Cole and his fiddlers three.

Hey Diddle Diddle

Hey diddle diddle,
The cat and the fiddle,
The cow jumped over the moon.
The little dog laughed
To see such fun,
And the dish ran away with the spoon.

The Owl and the Pussycat

by Edward Lear

The owl and the pussycat went to sea,
In a beautiful pea-green boat,
They took some honey and plenty of money,
Wrapped up in a five-pound note.
The owl looked up to the stars above,
And sang on a small guitar,
'O lovely Pussy! O Pussy, my love,
What a beautiful pussy you are, you are, you are,
What a beautiful pussy you are.'

Mary Mary, Quite Contrary

Mary, Mary, quite contrary,
How does your garden grow?
With silver bells,
And cockle shells,
And pretty maids all in a row.

Twinkle, Twinkle, Little Star

Twinkle, twinkle, little star, how I wonder what you are,
Up above the world so high,
Like a diamond
in the sky,
Twinkle, twinkle, little star,
How I wonder what you are.

Sing a Song of Sixpence

Sing a song of sixpence,
A pocket full of rye.
Four and twenty blackbirds,
Baked in a pie.

When the pie was opened,
The birds began to sing.
Now, wasn't that a dainty dish,
To set before the king?

The king was in his counting house,
Counting out his money.
The queen was in the parlor,
Eating bread and honey.

The maid was in the garden,
Hanging out the clothes,
When down came a blackbird
And pecked off her nose!

Row, Row, Row Your Boat

Row, row, row your boat,
Gently down the stream.
Merrily, merrily, merrily, merrily,
Life is but a dream.

60

Aaaahhh...

Row, row, row your boat,
Gently down the stream.
If you **see** a crocodile,
Don't forget to **scream**!

Hickory Dickory Dock

Hickory Dickory Dock,
The mouse ran up the clock,
The clock struck one,
The mouse ran down,
Hickory Dickory Dock.

Hickory Dickory Dock,
The bird looked at the clock,
The clock struck two,
Away she flew,
Hickory Dickory Dock.

Hickory Dickory Dock,
The dog barked at the clock,
The clock struck three,
Fiddle-de-dee,
Hickory Dickory Dock!

~ The End ~